WALT DISNEY
PICTURES PRESENTS

DINOSAUR
Aladar's Story

ADAPTED BY **Kathleen W. Zoehfeld**

ILLUSTRATED BY Disney Storybook Artists
Judith Holmes Clarke and Brent Ford
PAINTINGS BY John Alvin
DESIGN BY Dorit Radandt

Disney
PRESS

New York

I don't know who my parents were or where I came from, but for as long as I could remember, Lemur Island was my home. Plio says that one day a big egg just dropped out of the sky. The egg began to crack, and out I came!

The lemur clan became my family: Plio; her father, Yar; her daughter, Suri; and my best friend, Zini.

I grew bigger than anyone the lemurs had ever seen. But we all looked after one another. Life on Lemur Island was good. Until one night, when our whole world changed.

First a few streaks
of fire crossed the
sky. Then an
enormous fireball
crashed into
the sea!

My lemur family clung to my back, and we dodged a
hail of falling fire and crashing trees. Then a wave of fire
rolled toward us. I ran as fast as I could, barely staying
ahead of the flames.

At the island's edge, we leaped into the sea, just as the
wave engulfed the whole island.

We pulled ourselves ashore on the mainland and looked
back: our home had been destroyed.

The mainland was not much better. The watering holes had dried up, and there was nothing to eat—except us! A hungry pack of raptors thought we looked like a good meal!

The raptors were attacking, when suddenly the ground beneath us began to rumble. Out of a cloud of dust, a herd of huge creatures stomped toward us, and the raptors fled.

"STAY OUT OF MY WAY!" cried Kron, their leader.
"Look at all the Aladars!" gasped Suri.

As the Herd passed, an even bigger dinosaur, named Baylene, stopped and stared at the lemurs clinging to my back. "What an unfortunate blemish," she said.

"A good mudbath will clear those right up," added Eema as she walked by with her pet, Url.

"Um . . . they're my family," I said. "And my name's Aladar."

"Did I hear you say you were heading for your Nesting Grounds?" asked Plio.

"It's where the Herd goes to have their babies," explained Eema. "But that Fireball put us back a spell."

"We're being driven
unmercifully," added Baylene.
"We can hardly keep up."
When Kron lumbered past us
again, I asked: "Maybe you could slow
it down a bit?"
Kron sneered at my idea. His sister, Neera,
looked at me as if I were crazy.
These creatures who looked like me were a tough
bunch, but we could still see those raptors lurking
on the horizon. It was safer to stay with the Herd.

On and on we trudged through the desert with nothing to eat or drink. At last, Eema called out: "The lake! It's just over that hill, baby!"

But when we crested the hill, we stared out at a brown patch of dust and bones. The Fireball that had turned the land to desert had dried up the lake as well.

"The Nesting Grounds are only a few days away," shouted Kron. "Keep moving!"

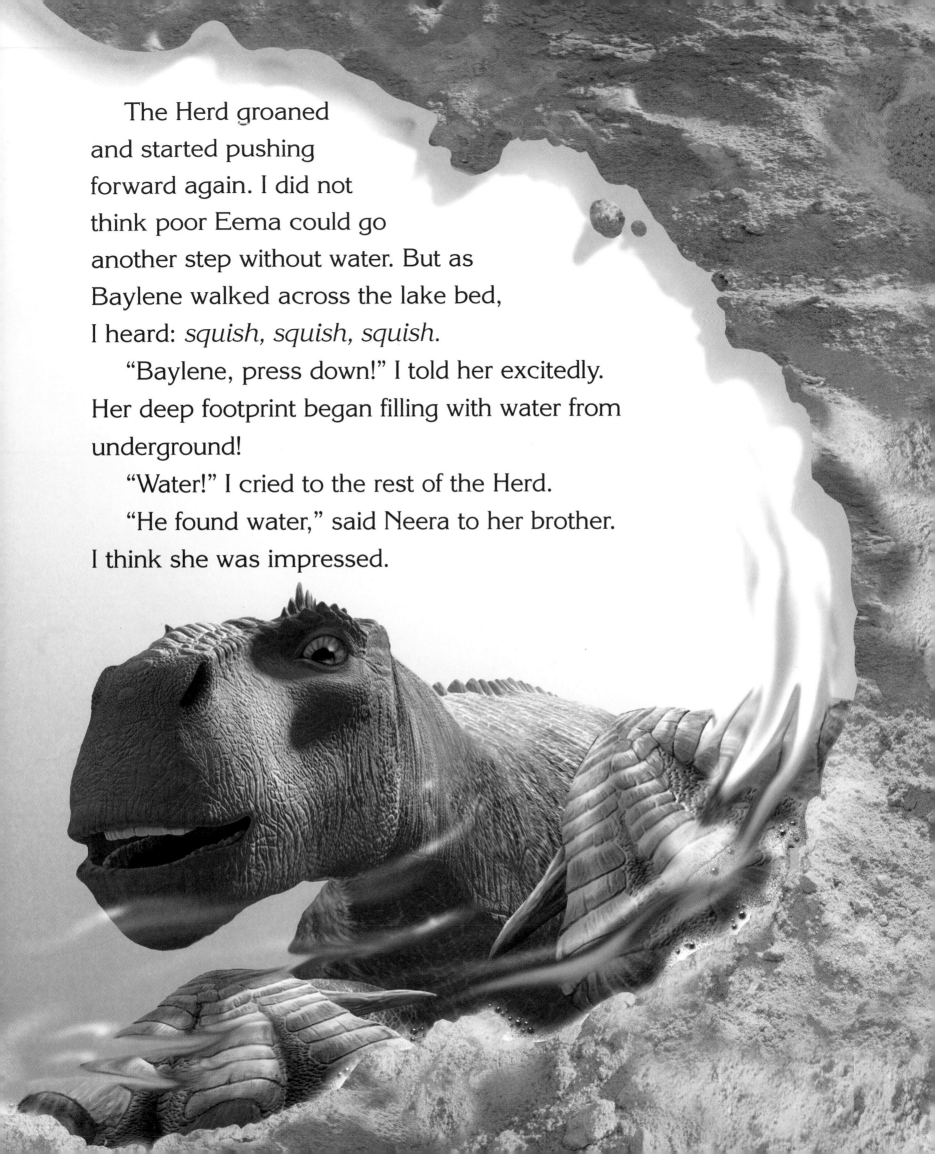

The Herd groaned
and started pushing
forward again. I did not
think poor Eema could go
another step without water. But as
Baylene walked across the lake bed,
I heard: *squish, squish, squish.*

"Baylene, press down!" I told her excitedly.
Her deep footprint began filling with water from
underground!

"Water!" I cried to the rest of the Herd.

"He found water," said Neera to her brother.
I think she was impressed.

Kron rushed back and
pushed me aside so he could be the
first to drink. Then the Herd went
wild—everyone pushing and
shoving for a place at the water.
Later that evening Neera asked
me: "Why did you help those old ones?"

"If we look out for each other," I explained, "we all stand a better chance of getting to your Nesting Grounds." Neera smiled at me.

But the moment did not last. We heard a terrifying roar in the distance: carnotaurs!

Carnotaurs were even more deadly than raptors.

"Move the Herd out!" cried Kron. He forced Neera along with him.

Kron drove the Herd at a fast pace.
My little group was left behind—alone
and lost.

As night fell, lightning cut across
the sky. We huddled in a cave.

We managed to get some rest,
but in the middle of the night, I
woke up. And there at the cave
entrance stood the carnotaurs!

"Eeeee!" squeaked Url.
One of the carnotaurs
pushed its toothy head in
through the cave's
entrance and sniffed.

We fled deeper and
deeper into the cave
and hoped for a
way out at the
other end.

Deep in the cave, Zini asked
eagerly: "Do you smell that?"
He had found fresh air! He climbed to the spot
where he felt the air coming in and started to dig.
I could see a ray of sunlight!
"Everybody stand back!" I cried. "We're outta
here." I started pushing on the rocks.
But the rocks just rumbled and shifted and
stuck even harder. No matter how I worked
and pushed, we weren't getting anywhere.
"We're not meant to survive,"
I said sadly.

"Oh, yes we are!" declared Baylene. She started pushing on those rocks with all her might, and my friends joined her. Their courage drove me on: I put my shoulder to the rock with the rest of them.

CRAAACCCK! Finally, the wall came tumbling down.

When the dust cleared, we could see before us a lush, green valley.

"The Nesting Grounds!" cried Eema.

"Our new home!" cheered Plio.

Next to Lemur Island, it was the most beautiful place I'd ever seen. But . . . "Where's the Herd?" I asked Eema.

"That is the way we used to get in here," said Eema, looking at a blockaded canyon. Neera and the others were trapped on the other side of a landslide!

As I raced back out of the cave, I spotted one of the carnotaurs again. I snuck away, hurrying to find the Herd before it was too late!

I found them at the mouth of the blocked canyon. Kron was trying to drive them up the rocky landslide. "A carnotaur is coming!" I shouted. "I know a new way to the valley. Follow me!"

"They're staying with me," growled Kron. He lunged at me and knocked me down!

Neera rushed to my rescue. With her
help, we drove Kron away. Soon,
though, we faced an even bigger
obstacle: the charging carnotaur!
I wondered—would the Herd
run away and try to follow Kron?
"Stand together!" I cried.
The Herd stood firm! They let out the
loudest, fiercest bellow I'd ever heard.
The carnotaur backed off. And, together,
we defeated him. The Herd bellowed in joy.

I showed them the way through the cave into the valley. We got there just in time for nesting.

Everyone helped Neera and me make a nest of our own. Our little nestlings were going to have the best bunch of grandparents any creatures could want.

From end to end, our valley rang with the happy sounds of families coaxing their babies into the world. I knew that life after the Fireball was not going to be easy. But in our journey here we had learned one thing for sure: we could do anything if we worked together!

For Liann — Kathleen Zoehfeld

For Colton Reed Clarke — Judie Clarke

For Sara, Nicholas, Melissa, and Lucas — Brent Ford

For Farah — John Alvin

Printed in the United States of America.

First Edition

ISBN 0-7868-3259-2
Library of Congress Cataloging-in-Publication Number: 99-68132

This book is set in 19-point Korinna.

For more Disney Press fun, visit www.disneybooks.com